AGE-OLD TALES
OF THE
GREEKS AND HEBREWS
ALTERED, *TWISTED* & MUTILATED
By Stanley Longman

**Age-Old Tales of The Greeks and The Hebrews:
Altered, Twisted & Mutilated**

Bilbo Books Publishing
www.BilboBooks.com

ISBN- 978-1-7326180-5-3

Printed in the United States of America

All rights reserved. Published in the United States of America by
Bilbo Books Publishing. Athens, Georgia

To contact Bilbo Books Publishing email bilbobookspublishing@gmail.com

Buon Viaggio

Longman's stories are here to stay. They are as new and startling as a look in the mirror, as old as mankind contemplating itself in Pleistocene art, biblical and Talmud tales and commentaries, Greek myths. In these fifteen powerful reflections, in part whimsical, ironic, tragic - even heartbreaking, tender and loving, enigmatic, Stan Longman does hold up a mirror to humanity, respectful of what he sees, like Rembrandt in his self-portraits with warts and wrinkles, but toward the end, with a smile.

Yet, Stanley, my friend for 70 years, sweet and lovable by nature, was born a true Doubting Thomas, totally aware of the contingencies of life, none the same from moment to moment, man to woman, man to man, god to god. His Age-Old Tales are at once a refreshing kick in the gut, not physical but philosophical, challenging the mind, and appealing to the heart. There is drama here as we might expect from a drama professor, but also humor, not ribald but joyful, playful like Weber's "Invitation to the Dance", or Leporello's inventories, or Figaro's comments on life as barber and as town gossip.

This is from a man whom I have loved as a fellow human and fellow humanist for some two generations, a linguist (Danish, Italian), raised on the Italian Renaissance at home and in Rome, Cortona and Parma, a master of the English language, who has used it here to give expression to tales, fables and metaphors that, as I said, will last. These are tales of the heavens and of earth, of heaven and hell, gods and angels, men and women, from the Pillars of Hercules, Athens to Jerusalem. For Stan Longman knows, better than most, that "the classics, including the major religious ones, are there for a reason, namely for a people to have a cultural skeleton on which to grow tissues and organs of all the values and virtues which once gave humankind civilizations so culturally essential as to endure thousands of years" (autem). Stan Longman gives voice in writing, as artists have done in painting or composers in music, to our human yearnings for love and understanding as a "*configurazione delle cose invisibili*".

These tales come of a "unique, personal vision, informed by an instinctual sense for truth that transcend[ed]s rational thought" (Longman, 2004). Thus: Hebrew vs. Greek? One or several Gods? Constrained or free or both? At Mass, I serve one. As biologist, one per species, while subspecies become my particular theological conundrum — a matter I will soon be taking up with Aquinas. Till then I stand with Longman: if God is not Life, then what is it? Is meaning to be extracted out of matter or bestowed on it? And so, we stand with the author in humility, continuing our search for meaning seen yet as dimly from Mount Nebo as from Mount Olympus.

John M. Opitz, Professor Emeritus
School of Medicine, University of Utah
January, 2020

Acknowledgements

Thanks to:
Clay Hulsey of Applied Images for layout design
Ursula Vogel for editing these tales
Bowen Craig and William Bray of Bilbo Books for publishing assistance

Table of Contents

Author's Note

There is something fascinating about the stories that have come down to us from two very different peoples, the Greeks and the Hebrews of the ancient world. The stories themselves appear at first very different and yet they grow out of the same impulse. Humanity has always sensed a mystery and wonder about the powers that work upon us. In particular, the myths and stories found in Greek mythology and in biblical stories were in response to that abiding, persistent feeling. Of course, these two peoples share the Mediterranean and it would not be beyond imagining that they might encounter one another from time to time. The myths also can provoke an urge to fill in details about how the narrative came about or how it might end.

So it is that the stories in this collection are of two sorts. Some are inventions of encounters between Greek characters and Hebrews. Examples include the account of how Odysseus met Jonah in the belly of the whale, how Adam and Eve met a woman with a box, and how Jason met Moses on the eastern shore of the Red Sea. Other stories enlarge on the originals. What might have happened if there had been a fourth magus who got separated from the three magi who visited the baby Jesus? One might wonder what led up to Joseph's encounter with Potiphar's wife and what followed it. Or we might suppose how the goddesses could revolt against the harassing behavior of the gods.

I intend these "altered, twisted and mutilated tales" as a tribute to the rich and provocative nature of the original stories. The new versions are indeed a reflection of the wonder generated by the originals. It is all part of the human predicament.

A Gathering of Goddesses

At one time a group of goddesses gathered on the lower slopes of Mount Olympus. Artemis called the meeting, motivated by her sense of outrage at the behavior of the gods. She was not alone in this. Several other goddesses appeared in response to her summons and they all had tales to tell. There were three who took particular interest in the discussion. Aphrodite found the exchange of stories quietly amusing while her little boy Eros darted in and out of the crowd carrying his bow and arrow. Athena offered few remarks, but she listened intently to all that was said. Finally, Hera had to be there for she knew many stories would feature her husband, Zeus.

Artemis led off with an account of her experience with the prying eyes of some lecherous hunter. The young man was hiding in the bull rushes near the pond where Artemis and some nymphs were bathing. They were all nude and had no idea they were being watched. Then suddenly the unfortunate young man made a sound that attracted attention. With some satisfaction, Artemis reported that she cast a spell on him causing him to transform into a stag. Immediately, his dogs attacked him viciously and tore him apart.

Some who listened to that story were startled for they knew of the disappearance of Actaeon but never knew of his death. Ignoring their protests, Artemis carried on, this time issuing a strong denunciation of the unchecked lechery of Zeus, who was constantly chasing after goddesses, nymphs, and women. He would often cast his roving eyes on female humans They somehow fascinated and enthralled him. Perhaps he enjoyed their variety, for there always seem to be new ones. And so it was that he would often descend to the earth to seduce mere mortal women.

Of course the gathered goddesses knew about this. Even Hera, his wife, knew about his escapades. Artemis stared at her for a moment and then launched into a new denunciation. This time however she took on a mocking tone. "You surely have heard the stories of how he would transform himself into a cloud, a shower of gold, a swan or a bull. It is as though he had no confidence in his ability to seduce on his own. It is really laughable."

From the far side of the crowd Aphrodite actually did laugh. She found all this amusing, a tribute to her power. Everyone turned and looked at her. "Well," she said. "Let me tell you about that shower of gold that came down on Danae lying in her bed. Can you imagine the scene? Danae wakes with a start as all variety of gold cascades over her. She is so startled, so amazed, she cannot realize that Zeus is having his way with her." And Aphrodite laughed again.

Then another goddess in the crowd called out, "What about Leda?" Suddenly a quiet came over the whole gathering. What indeed? Athena, who had been silent up to that moment, ventured a thought. "Zeus is my father. I was conceived in his brain and I caused him such pain that his head split open and I sprang out. Still for all that time in his brain, I have no way of accounting for how transforming into a swan could help him to seduce Leda. It must have to do with all that feathered fluttering." This produced another moment of silence as the goddesses considered that image. And again Aphrodite laughed.

Artemis turned to Hera to ask if she were aware of that episode. "Of course, as I have been aware of many of his sexual exploits. In this case my suspicions were confirmed when Leda laid an egg." Now Aphrodite guffawed. Hera ignored her and went on, "And when the egg hatched, out came Kastor and Pollux, the Dioskuro twins, looking much like their father."

Still addressing Hera, Artemis wondered about another animal that her husband had used. She was speaking, of course, of the bull who abducted Europa. "No, in that matter, I knew almost nothing, I shudder to think of it, but he carried her so far away across the sea, that I had no way of knowing how it ended." Hera paused at that moment, and then added, "I will tell you when I had a moment of vengeance in my own quiet way. This had to do with a beautiful human female named Io. Zeus transformed himself into a cloud and descended on the poor girl who was as startled and amazed as was Danae. Afterwards he tried to hide what he had done by spreading the cloud out over the land. When I caused the clouds to disperse, he immediately recognized I knew what he had done so he turned Io into a heifer, a beautiful white heifer. I told him how pleased I was with the heifer and asked him to give the creature to me. He couldn't do anything but grant my wish. So, I have had that beautiful animal in my stables ever since." Aphrodite laughed.

At this point, Eros, Aphrodite's boy, stepped away and looked down the slope of the mountain. "Is that not your brother, Apollo, seated on a boulder by the path?" Artemis looked down and said, with a note of affection, "Yes. That is my brother. The two of us have always been scrupulous in our behavior avoiding any form of luxuriant indulgence. We remain pure." Just then, a beautiful nymph, whom everyone recognized as Daphne, ran past Apollo. He stood up and followed her. Aphrodite nudged Eros who pulled out an arrow, placed a few drops on its tip and shot the arrow right at Apollo. He scarcely missed a step when the arrow struck him. He began to run faster. Daphne looked back over her shoulder and also ran faster. The faster he ran, the faster she ran. Still he was clearly gaining on her when Artemis stood up at her full height and cast a spell on Daphne. Just as Apollo was reaching out to wrap his arms around her body that body turned into the trunk of a laurel tree, standing now in a grove of laurel trees. Indeed she was a beautiful laurel tree. Apollo stumbled back in astounded frustration. One laurel tree standing close by, waved its limbs gently and seemed to whisper, "Me, too!" And again, Aphrodite laughed.

The FOURTH Magus

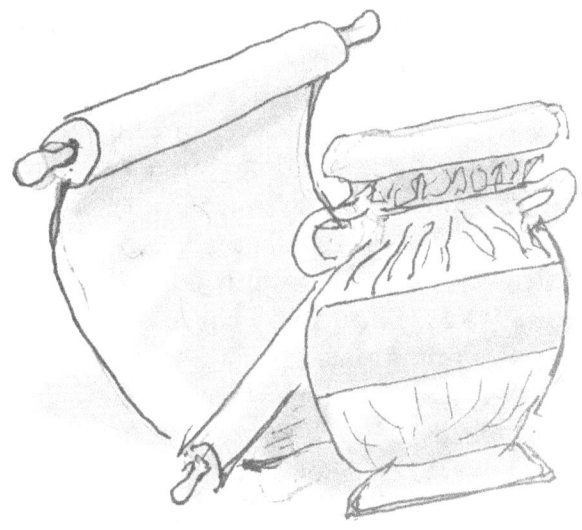

One day, more than two thousand years ago, there was an extraordinary meeting. It was an intertribal meeting called by the High Magus. It took place in Jerusalem and many of the most learned magi came. Some had to travel long distances to arrive at the congress center but there was ample reason for them to do so. Two very unusual events were happening in the heavens and they needed to consider the nature of these two events and what they might portend. One event had been predicted but the other was a surprise. The first was the conjunction of the planets Saturn and Jupiter. They were in perfect alignment. At the same time a powerful star had appeared. It seemed to have come from the farthest depths of the universe.

They conferred among themselves with more than a measure of anxiety. Surely the conjunction of Saturn and Jupiter was enough to cause the magi to search for what effect it might have here on earth, but the appearance of the bright star in the east was truly confounding. There were a few very old magi who recognized that this was not really a star. They had seen this happen many decades earlier. They went aside to confer and then they reported to the congress that this was a celestial body that had appeared many years ago and caused a great drought among the people of Israel. They hastened to add that this thing, called a comet (they remembered) need not portend disaster. On hearing this, others argued that its appearance coming with the conjunction of the planets would only double the chances for catastrophe.

This dispute went on for some time. Suddenly one of the magi, who was called Caspar and had come from India, stood up and spoke, saying, "God called to me. I listened and heard Him urge me to go where a star will point the way. If I do, I will come to a little town and there I would find a little child in a manger and that child will become Messiah and King." Then another magus, Balthazar from Babylon, stood and declared that God appeared to him with the same message. Two more magi, Melchior from Persia and Ohad from Midian, had the same divine announcement. When the other magi heard this, others at the congress mocked them, saying that it was all a shared hallucination or worse a conspiracy they had invented.

In this way, the Congress of Magi broke up, some convinced a plague would soon begin, others that a great flood such as Noah had endured would destroy the earth or perhaps flames so hot and so powerful that it will destroy all mankind. A few declared their belief that the heavenly spectacle promised God's blessing and a new covenant. The four magi gathered outside watching their colleagues disappear as they began their long journeys homeward. They stood there considering how they should proceed. Melchior looked into the sky and said, "I do believe that the star they called a comet is actually pointing our way. You see the light that goes out of the body of the star. That surely is pointing the way we should go."

They all concurred. Balthazar, however, offered this advice: "As we are here traveling through Judea, the land governed by Herod the Great, it behooves us according to proper protocol to do him homage."

"Is his palace anywhere nearby?" asked Caspar. As he was from India, he was not knowledgeable about this part of the world.

"It is indeed," said Ohad, who lived not so very far away. "It is here in Jerusalem and it rises high above the city. I know something of King Herod, too, and you do well to visit him for you can arouse his anger if you do things without his knowledge."

So, they gathered their belongings and saddled up their two horses and Balthazar's camel. Ohad rode with Balthazar and gave directions to the palace. And when they arrived, Herod himself invited them to his throne room, for he had heard about this child.

"Welcome learned gentlemen. You do me honor with this visit. I know that the Intertribal Congress of Magi has taken place in my Jerusalem."

"Your majesty," said Caspar, bowing before him as did the other three. "We are here to pay our respects and inform you that we will be traveling through your realm."

"I most happily grant you leave to travel wherever you must go. But tell me please, does this bright star in the eastern sky mean anything? Have the magi declared what it portends?"

"They are of two minds about it, your Highness. Some say there will be a disaster on earth, others insist it announces a coming blessing," Melchior answered.

"Ah!" King Herod raised his eyebrows. "And might that blessing come in the form of a child?"

"Yes."

"How can a mere child be a blessing of such importance that it would provoke this stellar announcement?"

"Oh well," Ohad blurted out. "He will be the Messiah, he will be a King." He immediately regretted saying this, for he thought the less Herod knew, the better.

"I see." King Herod mused, putting his fingertips together. "Where do you suppose this child can be found?"

"We truly do not know, your highness. We do believe it is somewhere to the south of here," said Balthazar.

"I tell you, then, that I would be most obliged if you would return here once you have found him and let me know where I must go to pay homage to this blessed child."

"This we will surely do. Now with your permission we beg to take our leave for we do not know how far we must go." So saying, Caspar bowed, as did the others. "Most certainly. I wish you good travel in my kingdom. Do not fail to give me word of the child's whereabouts." The king gave them a regal wave.

Three magi turned to leave. Ohad, however, abruptly announced his need to relieve himself before any further travel. King Herod ordered a servant to accompany the magus to the royal latrine located deep in the bowels of the palace. The others assured him they would wait outside with the horses and the camel.

The servant led Ohad through corridor after corridor, down steps through a large hall into more corridors and down further steps until at long last they arrived at the latrine, a large room with a long bench on three walls punctuated with keyhole openings at regular intervals. The servant left Ohad there and disappeared. When Ohad had done, he looked about. There was no one in sight. He tried to retrace his steps but soon became hopelessly confused. He wandered down many halls and up stairs and around various courtyards, but he simply could not find a way out.

Meanwhile, the other magi could wait no longer. They saddled up and resumed travel following where the comet's tail directed.

Eventually Ohad found someone who took him back to the throne room where Herod welcomed him and told him he would be his guest indefinitely until the others returned with the promised news of the child's location. They never did return. And so it was that Ohad remained a hostage and was never heard from again

Adam & Eve Out of the Garden

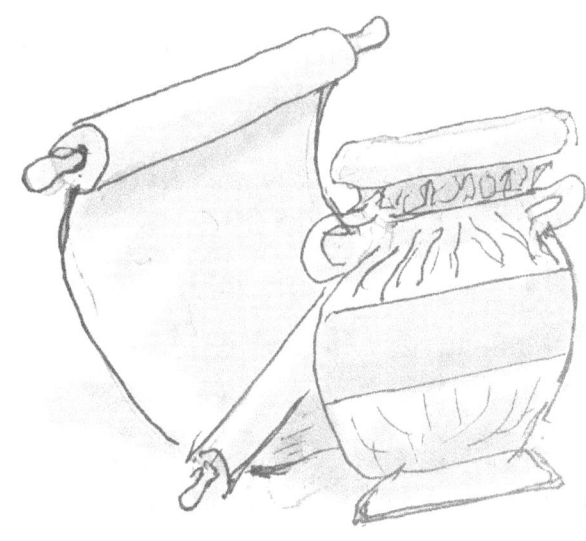

When God created Adam and Eve, He placed them comfortably in the Garden of Eden. He made sure they had everything they needed: sunshine, cool air, things to eat, as well as assurance and comfort such that they had no worries as to what it all meant. They were fully innocent. They revelled in life and it never occurred to them that life could come to an end. Nor did they concern themselves about whether their existence might carry some sort of significance. It simply did not matter. They lived and loved. They delighted in all the plants and animals that surrounded them.

There was one matter that created intense curiosity in them. It was about a tree. God had said that they may eat the fruit of any tree in the garden with one exception, and that was the Tree of Knowledge. That fruit was forbidden. Their curiosity about that fruit grew daily. Why, they wondered, should this be forbidden? Was it a particular juice contained in the fruit? Or was it pulp of the fruit? What could make it so special? Might it be something to do with that word, "knowledge"? They simply did not recognize that word.

At last they could stand the temptation no longer. Eve stood a long while below the boughs of that tree admiring the fruit that hung there. As she gazed up into the tree, she heard a soft soothing sound. It was the voice of a charming serpent wound around the limbs of the tree.

The serpent smiled, saying, "This fruit is surely beautiful to behold. I assure you it's delectable to taste. I suppose you have been told not to eat any of this fruit. Am I right?"

Eve nodded her head. "God said we must not eat of the tree in the middle of the garden. If we do, He said, we will surely die."

"Pfft!" the serpent hissed. "You most certainly will not die. What do you think He meant by that word, 'die'?"

"I don't know,"

"He is trying to scare you. To die means to cease to exist. You really think that would happen?"

"No."

"He simply does not want you to have knowledge because if you do, you will be like Him, you will be a god, too."

"Oh."

"Go ahead, have a bite," said the serpent nodding his head toward one particularly plump piece of fruit.

"Oh well, why not?" said Eve, reaching up and snatching the fruit. She bit into it. It was truly delicious. But as soon as she swallowed, her mind became very active. Immediately

she started thinking of all manner of things – things such as why she had been created, or what life means, or the strange shame she suddenly felt in her nakedness and what might lie outside the Garden.

She saw Adam approaching and she crossed her arms in front of her body. She told him what she had done. He of course was alarmed and reminded her of God's admonition not to eat of this fruit. She handed him the unfinished fruit saying, "Take it. Eat. It makes your mind do wonderful things."

"All of a sudden I found out what knowledge is. I realized that I am alive and that I may find meaning in my life. All sorts of other things came to mind, things that I never wondered about."

Adam was dubious. He looked up at the serpent who smiled and urged him on by nodding his head. Adam looked at the fruit in his hand and at Eve. "Why are you trying to hide your body with your arms?"

"Oh, I don't know. It comes from a feeling I got from the fruit. Go ahead. Try it."

He looked at her quizzically, then bit into the fruit. At once he had strange feelings much like those Eve experienced. He began to understand who he was, what life was meant to be, how he might express his ideas and visions. He was consumed with curiosity about the world beyond the garden and how he might go out there to explore. And he cupped his hand over his crotch. It was as if all things that had seemed natural now took on a new and complex aspect.

Of course, it was not long before God began calling for Adam. And Adam hid himself in the bushes. Finally, Adam answered, saying that he was ashamed in his nakedness. God knew exactly what had happened. And it alarmed Him that both Adam and Eve now had full knowledge of the truth. He issued His curse that they will always toil to cultivate the earth and they will both return to dust from which they were created. Then a fiery angel appeared and drove them out the portal into the world beyond Eden.

Outside they marveled at all that they seemed to have suddenly known and now forgot. It puzzled them and they each tried to recall truth. Meanwhile, however, they quickly found leaves large enough to clothe themselves. They began a hard life of labor and uncertainty. They worked the earth and saw it yield crops. But at the end of each day they would collapse in exhaustion. They would sink into a deep slumber and in that slumber something very mysterious would happen. It happened to each of them. One or the other would seem to be inside a darkened chamber facing a dimly lit screen on which they could discern only shadowy and amorphous images floating about. From time to time an image or a figure or a set of words became clear and then faded way.

They had lost most of the understanding they had gained from the Tree of Knowledge but they could return to the chamber to gain some new understanding. As they watched and glimpsed those clear images, they were startled for in those moments they recalled the reality they once knew so well but now only in a sketchy way.

Eventually, many children were born. And their progeny also witnessed these things. Mankind became restless to discover truth and understand reality. And out of all this came religion, philosophy, metaphysics, epistemology, aesthetics, ethics – all those avenues humanity has pursued in the search for truth. To this day the search for meaning has gone on without cease.

Adam & Eve meet a Woman with a BOX

The Lord set a test for the newly created humans, Adam and Eve. They were placed in a paradise and allowed full freedom to explore and enjoy all its wonders. Everything about this garden called Eden was pleasant and refreshing. The sweet air floated in balmy breezes. There was an abundance of nutritious and delicious foods. They loved and admired each other. In almost every way they experienced deep contentment – except for one worry. Perhaps it was not a worry but more a nagging temptation to eat the forbidden fruit of the tree in the center of the garden. Every time they passed that tree, they would stop to look at it, wonder about it and sniff its aroma.

Of course, it is generally known that they eventually succumbed to the temptation. Suddenly all that had seemed beautiful to them became ugly or bitter. They found their bodies a source of shame and hid from the Lord. He found them and, in His anger, had His avenging angel drive them out of Eden.

Simultaneously, the great god Zeus had taken umbrage against Prometheus for his presumptuous assertion of his will. He especially aroused the god's ire by inventing fire and sharing it with humans. As a result, Zeus had him chained to a rock and sent birds to eat at his liver daily. That was not enough. He then chose to place a temptation on humankind through Prometheus' brother, Epimetheus. He had Hephaestus fashion a beautiful woman and gave her to Epimetheus as a gift along with a locked box. Zeus warned both of them never to open that box. Epimetheus took the woman for his wife, put the box aside and placed the key in a safe place.

The woman, whose name was Pandora, knew where the key was placed. She took the box and the key out into the world. She looked for a distant spot where she could sit comfortably and examine the mysterious box. That spot was just outside a magnificent portal that led into Eden. For a long while she looked at that box and considered what precious items might be inside. Then, ever so tentatively, she unlocked the box and opened the lid just a crack. Suddenly a serpent thrust its way out of the box and slithered under the doors of the portal, disappearing into Eden. Pandora immediately slammed the lid down. She was in a state of shock. For a very long time she sat there holding the closed box. Eventually she became sleepy and dozed off.

Then a strange thing happened. The doors of the portal were thrown open. Pandora awoke with a start and saw a fiery angel fly over two people forcing them out. The two stumbled forwards in abject sadness. It was all over in a shot. The angel withdrew and flew back inside as the doors slammed shut. Of course those two people   were Adam and Eve. Pandora stood up and greeted them. They were slow to respond after the horrendous experience they had just suffered. They stood there trying to cover their nakedness. Meanwhile Pandora attempted to speak soothing words to comfort them.

Eventually curiosity got the better of Pandora and she inquired as to what lay on the other side of that portal. Eve described the beauty of the garden where they had lived so peacefully. That impressed Pandora. She stood there admiring the portal and imagining the wonders on the other side.

Then Adam pointed to the box that sat on the ground behind Pandora. He asked, "Does that box belong to you?"

Pandora stuttered, "Yes, yes. Yes, it does. It belongs to me and to my man. Zeus gave it to us and said it must not be opened. But I could not stop myself and I took it here away from home. I tried to resist the temptation, but then I opened it ever so slightly. Suddenly, out came a serpent. It slithered under the doors there and disappeared. I slammed the lid shut for fear something else might come out. Did you see a serpent back there in that garden?"

Eve of course had to admit that she had. And she recounted for Pandora how she encountered the smooth-talking serpent who tempted her to eat the forbidden fruit. "Adam ate of the fruit as well. Now we have been expelled and cursed. Even the serpent was cursed."

Pandora watched the pair trudge away leaving her and her box behind. She studied that box. She thought about what good things might be inside. She said to herself: "Now that the serpent is gone and even cursed, it might be safe to open." Feeling reassured, she slowly opened the box but the lid was thrown back and all variety of vermin, winged creatures, snarling hairy monsters, lizards, swarming insects, and screeching birds flew up into the air. Some chased after Adam and Eve, others hovered over Pandora. All of them together created a deafening cacophony. She cowered, her arms wrapped over her head. Eve looked back at Pandora accusingly. This was clearly a spectacle of unbridled evil.

In the midst of that mayhem, something very different happened. Pandora heard a gentle cooing sound coning from somewhere in the box. Very tentatively, she looked inside and saw a white bird at the bottom of the box. She reached in and brought forth a gentle bird that flew high up in the air. Adam, Eve and Pandora watched it swoop this way and that among the swarming little beasts. And as it fluttered above them, it had the effect of scattering those creatures. They did not actually disappear but they became much less menacing. It was the bird of hope and it infused in all three a sensation of peace. That did not put them at ease, for worry, fear, and horror still played in their minds, but hope did lend them a measure of courage.

The Amazing LIFE of Melchizedek

This account begins with Melchizedek's birth. That in and of itself is amazing. His mother, Sofonim, was a virgin. She was also the wife of Nir who chose to delay consummation of the marriage for reasons that remain mysterious and unknown. Some have argued that it was a part of God's plan. Sofonim died at the moment of Melchizedek's birth. He himself sat on the bed next to the corpse. As he sat there, he was suddenly fully grown, fully clothed and fully articulate. He spoke a blessing. And he prayed, offering thanks to the Lord. There and then, the Lord anointed him High Priest on earth. He then turned to Nir who stood there in wonder and grief. And Melchizedek interceded with the Lord on his behalf and the Lord gave comfort.

In this manner, Melchizedek went out into the world working for lost souls, granting them forgiveness, and assuring them of God's love. He himself became much beloved. But then there came a day when rain began to pour down on the earth. For days and days, it continued. Melchizedek recognized the growing flood came from God's displeasure with the behavior of mankind, so much so that there was no longer forgiveness. He also saw his uncle Noah (Nir's brother) at work on a large boat. Seeing that work going forward, Melchizedek ran to find his father Nir. When he found him, the water had already risen and one could see the arc floating on the waters off in the distance. On board were Noah, his wife, their three sons and their wives, but there was no room for Nir. He was not bitter or angry. He felt his sins had mounted to a level that he did not deserve to be saved. Melchizedek would not accept that and he ran and found a rowboat with oars and had Nir get in. Once cast off into the water, Nir began to row, looking back at his son with tears in his eyes. Then he heard his son shout that he should not worry for he will be saved.

As he rowed the boat, without any sense of where he could go, he came upon two curious sea creatures. They had just broken the surface of the water. Nir could hear them talking. They were of a species, now extinct, fully capable of talking to one another. They complained bitterly about the unending rain that was so diluting the seawater that many fish were dying. Nir came close to them in his boat and joined in the conversation. While they were discussing this unfortunate state of affairs, they all looked up and observed a large winged creature carrying a man above the surface of the great waters. They had never seen anything like that. It was a spectacle very much like an eagle carrying off its prey. In puzzlement they turned to Nir, asking if he could explain what they just saw.

He knew what must have happened, for his son had told him of such matters. He told them, "What you just saw was an archangel."

They asked at once, "What is an archangel? Never saw anything like that bird. Are there many of them?"

"No, no. In fact, there aren't more than about four or five of them. That one might have been Michael. They serve the Lord in His dealings with men."

"Is this Michael bird going to do something awful to that man he's carrying?"

"That man is my son. And I am sure that God has called on the archangel to take him to safety."

"We cannot imagine where he can find safety in this horrific flood. It's everywhere." Saying that, the two sea creature dove down out of sight.

After that for a long while, Nir bobbed on the waters in his little boat. He gave up rowing because he had nowhere to go. But then he looked out to the distant horizon and perceived what seemed to be the archangel coming toward him. And he was. Suddenly the archangel swooped down and plucked Nir out of his boat. Flapping his great wings, he took off in the direction he had come. They flew together for a great while and eventually came to an imposing portal. This was the Garden of Eden that somehow stood up out of the great flood. In front of the portal stood Melchizedek to welcome his father. It was a moment of sheer joy.

Once the waters receded, and after a white dove flew over carrying an olive branch, Melchizedek and Nir spotted Noah's great ark in the distance settled on the peak of Mount Ararat. As the land replaced the water, the Garden of Eden faded from view and the two, father and son, stepped down on the earth. Melchizedek interceded with God the Father on behalf of his own father, causing the two brothers, Noah and Nir, to be reunited.

From that time forward, Melchizedek walked the earth dispensing forgiveness, assuring the people of God's grace, and spreading peace. Some have surmised that he was indeed Jesus Christ come to earth only to return many centuries later to do the work that he as Melchizedek had begun. There is no record of his death and it well may be that he is still among us.

In The Belly of The Whale

This story, a lost chapter of the Odyssey, tells of the meeting of Odysseus and Jonah.

While Odysseus was sailing for Phaeacia from the Isles of Ogygia on a raft he had made to escape the fair goddess, Calypso, Poseidon was returning from Ethiopia. Standing on the far-off mountains of the Solymi, he espied Odysseus rowing on the wine dark sea. The shaker of the earth caused the sea to toss tempestuously and thereby smashed the raft of Odysseus, for Poseidon sought vengeance for the blinding of the one eye of his son, Polyphemus, the Cyclops. When Poseidon saw Odysseus wallow in the raging sea, he laughed aloud and caused the waves to mount up all the more.

So those mighty waves tossed Odysseus mercilessly. Now as he rose to the top of one monstrous wave, he espied a ship bobbing at a small distance. When he called out to the ship, the roaring thunder of the tempest swallowed up his voice and no one on the ship heard it nor did anyone take note of him.

But then Odysseus beheld a man cast into the sea. And suddenly the sea ceased its great turmoil. With great curiosity he swam towards the man who had been cast from the ship. But when he drew nigh unto him, a monstrous whale arose out of the deep and, with its jaws wide apart, swallowed up the poor man. Yet while Odysseus was unsure what had happened, for it happened so very quickly, the whale turned about and swallowed him also.

Now when Odysseus passed through the whale's mouth and came into its belly, a voice spake forth out of the darkness and bade him welcome. Odysseus was surely pleased to have company in that darkness within the belly of the whale. Odysseus then spake in the direction of that voice to inquire who had so welcomed him.

The voice uttered this reply: "Yea, verily, I am sad Jonah of the Hebrews and I have gone forth from the presence of the Lord. Lo, the Lord caused the sea to toss so frighteningly that the men on board sought to find out whose sins had brought the sea into such powerful turmoil. And they cast lots to see who was at fault with the Lord. And yea the lot fell upon me. They turned to me asking 'What shall we do so that the Lord might cease the sea's raging?' And I replied. 'Throw me in the sea for then surely will the waves stop their turmoil.' But they were loath to do so. Yet though they continued to smite the waters with their oars, they could bring the ship no closer to land. And when they saw they could bring the ship no closer to land, they turned to me, recalling what I had told them. So, then they cast me overboard into the sea. At once the Lord caused the raging waters to cease. In that way my shipmates were saved. But then arose this great whale that swallowed me whole. Now behold, here I am, the Lord your God."

Now the voice out of the darkness caused Odysseus great wonderment. Many questions rose up in his mind. After pondering some while, he asked sad Jonah, "Who is this Lord you speak of? Do you call Poseidon 'Lord'?"

Sad Jonah made reply: "I speak of the Lord my God. I have no knowledge of that Poseidon you speak of."

"It was he, the god of the sea, that caused the tumultuous waves. Now, how can you go forth out of his presence?" Odysseus wanted to know.

Jonah then told how the Lord had come before him and ordered him to go to the great city of Nineveh and cry out against it for the wickedness it had fallen into. Unless they repent their evil, He would destroy the city and all its people. Jonah paused, then said, "But I was exceedingly afraid. Therefore, I made my way to Joppa and there I found a ship bound for Tarshish. And from that ship was I cast forth into the sea."

"This Lord you call your God is an angry and vengeful god. But what had the people of Nineveh done to cause such anger?"

"Yea verily, have they been wicked."

"Wicked unto the Lord?"

"Nay, wicked amongst themselves," replied sad Jonah.

Now Odysseus was much puzzled for he could not reason why wickedness amongst themselves should cause such anger in this Lord, Jonah's God. But before he could ask about this wonderment, Jonah inquired how it came to pass that Odysseus found himself there in the belly of the great whale.

Then with just pride, Odysseus of many counsels related the long story of his wanderings in search of his home in Ithaca after the fall of Troy. Jonah was much surprised to learn that Odysseus was the son of Laertes of the seed of Zeus. Odysseus recounted how he came to the Isles of the Lotus-eaters whence his men were loath to leave because of the effects of the lotus, and how he blinded the one eye of Polyphemus and thereby incurred the wrath of Poseidon, and how he came to the island of Circe who turned his men into swine. Further did Jonah hear how Odysseus had sailed past the sirens and how a shipwreck brought him alone to the Isle of Ogygia where the fair goddess Calypso kept him from leaving as she had such love for him. Jonah marveled that a goddess might love a man. Finally, Odysseus told how he escaped Calypso's island on a raft when Poseidon caught sight of him and, in his anger, caused the rocking of the sea.

Now Jonah marveled at the many courageous deeds he heard from the mouth of Odysseus. Even more did he marvel at the vengeful nature of this god Poseidon. Then he spake, saying, "Behold, we are here together in the belly of this great whale and the waters encompass us around. Let us now pray unto our gods, each to his own, promising sacrifices unto them lest we remain forever in this abominable belly of hell."

Thus spake Jonah and Odysseus assented. They each prayed to their gods, even deep in the whale's belly, they prayed. Now, Odysseus of many counsels and sad Jonah were in the belly of the whale three days and three nights. When the rosy-fingered dawn of the fourth day shone forth, the whale swam nigh unto the shore. And there the whale vomited forth the two of them. In this manner they came into the land of the Hebrews. They washed themselves in the waters of the sea and stretched themselves upon the sand of that beach where they both fell into a deep slumber.

Now, Jonah awoke suddenly having heard the voice of the Lord who reprimanded him, saying, "Arise, go to Nineveh, that great city, and do the preaching I bade you do that the people might turn from their wicked ways." So, Jonah jumped to his feet. He shook Odysseus saying, "The Lord my God has spoken to me in my dream. Therefore, I must needs go straightway to Nineveh." Saying so, he started out.

But Odysseus stopped him. "I am a stranger here in this land. If it please you, let me come even to the city of Nineveh, for I would search out what manner of men live in that great city."

And so it was that the two went forth from that beach and made their way to Nineveh. As soon as they entered the city gates, Jonah straightway began to cry out, declaring for all to hear: "Yet forty days and Nineveh will be overthrown." Some were deeply ashamed for their many misdeeds and evil ways, but others turned away and would not listen. Odysseus himself was hard pressed to recognize how dire the city's fate might be. Yet there were indeed so many acts of cowardice, greed, and violence that he saw truth in Jonah's words. And it was with time that Jonah brought the people to take stock of their wickedness. They then cast away their worldly belongings and donned sackcloth, yea even the richest among them. The king of Nineveh, even he, rued his many sins, cast off his royal robes, covered himself with sackcloth and proclaimed a fast in the city.

Now Odysseus of many counsels was a man of great cunning. Observing that the royal palace was left open, he went to the King and offered to care for the palace in the King's absence during the time of the city fast. Odysseus turned and entered the palace by its front gate. Once inside he ordered the servants to prepare a great feast. When the many dishes were brought to the table, he paused to make prayers to Athena and to Poseidon, for he hoped for the continued favor of the one and the forgiveness of the other. He offered no prayers to Dionysus, whose powers hold sway over food and drink. And so it happened that just as Odysseus raised the goblet of wine to his lips, every last item on the table vanished and the table remained bare.

So also did it come to pass that the aromas from the royal kitchen wafted forth from the palace. The people were exceedingly annoyed for their bellies bade them eat. Recalling the words of Jonah, they resisted the temptation to rush into the palace. But they took counsel among themselves for they worried that the wrath of God might come down upon them solely because of Odysseus' gluttony in the midst of their fast. Therefore, they determined to drive him from their great city. But when they approached the palace gate, the servants fled from within, crying out how the whole feast had magically vanished. The crowd heard from them how they were kept from the penitential city fast because of Odysseus' orders. Now they all murmured among themselves that a demon might have done these things. So, was it determined that they should drive Odysseus out of the palace and out of the city itself.

As this was happening, thundering laughter filled the halls as Dionysus mocked Odysseus and drove him out the back gate. There he thanked the gods that no one had seen him, made his way to the city gates and there, with his agile speed, ran out into the countryside beyond. There at last, greatly relieved, he laid himself under a tree to rest. And so it was that he fell into a deep slumber.

When the rosy-fingered dawn of the next morning awakened Odysseus, he looked about himself. At some distance he espied his companion Jonah lying beside a wilting plant. Odysseus rose and went across to join him, curious as to how he came to be so far out of the city. And so he inquired and Jonah answered: "I came forth out of the city and sat upon this hillside to watch the Lord wreak destruction upon Nineveh. But the Lord spake again to me with these words: 'I have seen the works of these people, that they have turned from their evil ways and I repent the destruction of the city that I had threatened.' Lo this caused me great anger, for the Lord my God had taken the truth from my mouth that Nineveh should be overthrown. Then the Lord saw my anger and created this plant to grow up and shield me from the heat of the day and then caused the plant to wither at the sun's hottest moment."

"And did that rekindle your anger against that Lord your God?" asked Odysseus.

"Yea, it did just so. And the Lord instructed me, saying: 'Why should you be angry about the plant which I created and which I destroyed? Should you not rather pity the plant for which you did not labor? Should I not pity Nineveh for which you did labor?'"

"And were you then reconciled?"

"Yea, so I do believe," replied Jonah.

Then Odysseus recounted how he displeased his god Dionysus who took vengeance on him for ignoring him in his prayers at the banquet table. It was that curse that caused the food to vanish and the servants to run away. It was also that curse that caused the god's laughter to drive Odysseus out of the palace.

Jonah chided Odysseus, declaring: "When you went straight into the palace and called for a feast to be prepared, I was alarmed fearing you would bring the wrath of God upon us. But then we were spared. The aromas of your feast placed temptation before the people of Nineveh and yet at the last they resisted. And the Lord my God saw that -- and He was pleased."

Hearing the words Jonah had spoken, Odysseus rose to his feet, saying, "Would that Dionysus my god were pleased also!"

Jonah looked up at Odysseus and replied thus: "This Dionysus and that other one, Poseidon, seem petty, self-centered and jealous. They want nothing but attention and grow angry if they do not get it. Are all your gods like that?"

Now Odysseus thought on this and then said. "Jonah, you must see that nature is cruel and its many forces call for obeisance. Otherwise great and frightful things can come down out of the heavens."

"The Lord my God is a righteous god," Jonah replied. "He brings down His wrath only to punish the wicked."

Odysseus sighed. "As for wickedness, we must work that out for ourselves. We must reason about what makes a good life. The gods will not tell us."

Then he added, "Jonah, my newfound friend, we have been through a trying time. The gods wield such power over us that our only recourse is humility."

Jonah nodded his assent: "I know I can turn to the Lord my God for help and support. And yet I know He may even then treat me harshly. And so, I too humble myself."

Jonah stood with Odysseus and they both looked back on Nineveh. Odysseus remarked thus: "It is a marvel that great city still stands."

So saying, Odysseus bade Jonah farewell and started off on the road to Joppa where he might find a ship to take him to Phaeacia or even to Ithaca, his home. To help him find his way, Athena, in the guise of a fisherman, walked with him. Jonah watched them move off and wondered where that fisherman came from and who he might be. And then he shook his head and turned his steps toward home.

a FALLEN Angel

The young shepherd Obediah ran into the main square of his little town. He ran as fast as his legs would carry him all the way proclaiming in a loud voice words such as "Wonderful!" "Amazing!" "I saw it myself!" "It was terrible!" By the time he got into the square, he was so out of breath that he couldn't answer the people saying, "What was wonderful? What was amazing? What was terrible? WHAT did you see?" The townspeople were used to Odediah's tendency to excited exaggeration, so they were ready to dismiss whatever he had to report. This time, however, he had a more urgent sense about him -- he might really have something to report. So, they waited for him to stop gasping.

When he had recovered, he looked intensely at the people gathered around him. Then he said to them, "Do you think it is possible to lose your footing when you are in heaven? I mean, lose your footing and fall to the earth? Could that happen?"

Of course, that puzzled people. Why, they wondered, should he ask that? Then, someone offered to bring the Rabbi and ask him. They did send for the Rabbi, who came and explained that it would be highly improbable. The only event remotely like that was the fall of Lucifer and his mutinous crowd of angels. "But," he added, "those angels fell into the underworld where they founded a new and evil empire. They might visit the earth. In fact, they often do just to spread dissension and mayhem. But they never fell to the earth. That's preposterous!"

"Well," said Obediah quietly. "I saw it happen out in my pasture."

"What?   What are you saying?"

"I'm saying, I saw an angel fall from the sky. He must have come out of heaven. He landed right next to the sheepfold. He's lying out there in the pasture with the feathers of his wings spread out around him. Somehow, I don't think he's going to get up and fly away. If you think I am making this up, come out and look for yourselves."

There was much chatter among the crowd. Finally, a few, including the Rabbi, told him to show them the way. And they all went off following Obediah out of the town and to the pasture. There, sure enough, they found what seemed an angel lying on his back, his wings spread out on the ground, mostly just feathers. They certainly were in no condition to lift the angel up and fly him away. What's more, the angel seemed dead.

That caused a bit of a stir in the crowd. One turned to the Rabbi and asked him if angels die. The answer came right back: "Of course not. Angels are immortal. They don't die."

"So, this is not an angel?" Obediah asked.

"Can't you see? That is no spiritual being. That is a man in flesh and blood. I suppose we are going to have to bury him even though we have no idea of his name."

Obediah was still puzzled: "How did he get up in the sky? That's where he came from. I saw him tumble from way up high. Doesn't make sense."

The Rabbi shrugged. "Oh well, the world always will have its mysteries."

People were silent as they pondered this. Eventually they developed a plan. They would get a gurney and carry this poor man-angel to the cemetery and give him a proper burial. So, they started to carry out that plan. They returned to the town and found a gurney. Some undertook to dig a grave while others went back to the pasture. They lifted the man-angel up onto the gurney and scattered the feathers. The men lifted the gurney and marched with it toward the town.

Before they got close to the town gates, a man stepped in front of the little parade and demanded they stop. They did as he said. They put the gurney down. The man knelt down beside the man-angel and stared at the face for some time and then he began to sob.

The Rabbi was immediately concerned. "Sir, you seem to know this mam for you are clearly grieving there beside him. Can you tell us who he is? We simply want to give him an honorable burial."

The man looked up his eyes brimming with tears. He managed to choke out a few words: "He is my brother…my name is Iapyx, son of Daedalus." Then looking again on the face of his brother, he managed to announce the name: "This is Icarus."

Nobody in the crowd knew who Icarus was. Iapyx stood and he thanked the good people of the town for their honoring Icarus with a proper burial. They lifted the gurney and resumed their march to town. On the way, Iapyx told them how it came to pass that his brother fell out of the sky. "Our father, Daedalus," he explained, "is always inventive and sometimes creates weird projects. He discovered a way the fashion wings using feathers and wax. He and my brother worked on that together. I really wanted no part in it, but it worked. They both flew up into the sky. I confess I admired it Despite Father's warning, Icarus flew too close to the sun and the sun melted the wax holding the feathers together. And he fell back to earth."

That created a murmur in the crowd as they now envisioned how all this happened. When they arrived at the cemetery, Iapyx finished the story. Daedalus, the father, returned to earth and landed in Sicily. He calculated where Icarus might have landed and determined it had to be somewhere at the eastern end of the Mediterranean. So it was that Iapyx set out and arrived in the land of the Hebrews where he at last found his brother and witnessed his solemn burial in that remote land.

IN THE HOUSE OF
Potiphar

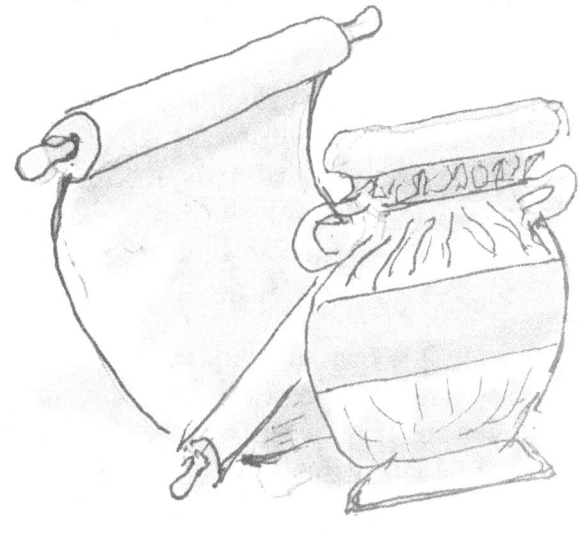

In Pharaoh's wondrous world of palaces, garrisons, stables, gardens, and ornate monuments, there was ample room for advancement into administrative posts that provided handsome salaries and perks. A gentleman by the name of Potiphar served as Captain of the Horse Guard, a post that allowed him to amass a considerable sum of money. He lavished much of it on his palatial residence. There came a time when he began to weary of all the details associated with his administrative work.

It was then that he met a slave dealer. The man sang the praises of a young man who seemed to have some sort of divine inspiration that enabled him to accomplish truly remarkable deeds. The dealer elaborated: "Indeed, I tell you I sense in him a kind of intuitive intelligence that would make him a wonderful household slave. I assure you this young man has a keen mind, organizing skills and knowledge of languages. Think of this: here's a man who could take on many of the responsibilities you shoulder right now. They could be shifted over to this slave." Still Potiphar hesitated.

The dealer watched him and, after a moment, made an offer: "I tell you what, seeing as it's you. I'll give you a five percent discount if you take him today. Here, I'll run and get him and let you look him over. If you don't like him after a week, turn him back to me and I'll refund your money. How about that?" Saying that, he ran off.

He returned instantly leading the slave. Potiphar noted that he was handsome and well-built, but he tested him on languages and on mathematics and on mental puzzles. He smiled. This really could provide him some relief from his day-to-day duties. And so it was settled. Money changed hands and the dealer left, only to return at once to say that the young man's name was Joseph.

Potiphar was pleased. He and Joseph talked together. Then Potiphar took the man on a tour of the palace and the barracks. They visited every room and garden. At the end Potiphar showed Joseph a study with a desk, a place where accounting and planning could be calculated. After that they went to the apartment where Joseph was to live.

Over the next few weeks, Joseph became acquainted with the many people who made up the administrative staff of the Horse Guard. He also assumed more and more responsibilities in maintaining records, issuing reports, doing the accounts and payroll. Potiphar took pleasure in visiting with him from time to time. He seemed to feel a sort of liberation from the dull routine he had had to follow. It was a load off his shoulders Joseph, for his part, was pleased to be of use.

Joseph was by all accounts a very handsome man. Nevertheless, he was surprised how often women turned their gaze on him and sometimes made gentle, suggestive remarks. One woman in particular seemed to single him out and brush up against him. In the midst of all this attention, he turned to a new friend named Aristides. He was a Greek but also a slave.

"I see you are puzzled and a little uncomfortable with all this attention. Surely it has happened to you before. Anyway, you must try to keep your eyes focused ahead. Try not to return their looks. If you do, you may very well lose control."

"There is one who is more forceful. She puts herself in my path. It's impossible to ignore her."

"Ah, that one! She is a siren."

"What do you mean, a 'siren'?"

"Oh, well, when we Greeks sail out toward the Pillars of Hercules, we pass a rocky island near Scylla. It's a dangerous place because of a race of women who enchant sailors with their ethereal voices causing them to smash their boats on the rocks. We call them sirens. They have a power strong enough that Odysseus put bees wax in his sailors' ears and bound himself to the ship mast to resist their power. We too bind ourselves to the masts of our ships or clap our hands over our ears."

"It won't do me any good to clap my hands over my ears. Yesterday she cupped her hand and squeezed my buttock."

"I think I know who that is. Her name is Zuleikha. I can only urge you to do everything you can to avoid her. She is Potiphar's wife." Aristides winked.

This was stunning news. Joseph did all he could to see to it any passageway he went into was empty. But still there were surprises. She came up behind and blew gently in his ear. On another occasion she pulled his hand to her breast. All through this, Potiphar continued to visit Joseph and consult on administrative matters. Of course, there was never any mention of Zuleikha. So far as Joseph knew, Aristides might have been teasing him by saying she was Potiphar's wife.

One day a servant came to Joseph's office to escort him to a room in the palace where an important dignitary needed to speak with him. Joseph put on his official cloak and followed him down several passageways he had never before seen. They came to a door which the servant opened. Then the servant ushered, almost pushed, Joseph in and disappeared at once.

Joseph turned to behold Zuleikha lying languidly on her bed. With one hand, she pulled on his waistband to bring him closer. With her other she flung the covers off, revealing herself fully naked. When she reached for his crotch, he turned and bolted from the room, letting his cloak fall to the ground as he fled.

In his horror and confusion, Joseph ran unsure of where he was going. In the distance he could her scream from her room. He ran faster although he truly did not know where to go. By chance, he encountered Aristides, his Greek friend. He helped him find his way home and then sat with him to console and comfort him. They both knew full well that this was going to finish badly.

Word came to Potiphar who went immediately to his wife. She showed him Joseph's cloak that he left behind when she screamed and drove him from her bed chamber. Potiphar was furious. He demanded someone go find Joseph at once. And when Joseph was brought before his master, he heard the sentence laid out for him: he was to be executed for the crime of rape. There was a moment of silence broken when Zuleikha urged her husband not to be so severe. He looked at her as a shadow of doubt crept over him. After another few moments of silence, he ordered Joseph to be thrown into the dungeon.

After only a brief time in the prison, Joseph endeared himself to the warden who happily had him undertake some of the guard duties. From time to time Aristides would visit. On one such occasion, he informed Joseph of a rumor circulating in the palace suggesting that everyone, including Potiphar, was convinced that Zuleikha had lied. Just a few days later, in fact, Potiphar ordered Joseph's release. They returned to their work together, but there was never any mention of the problem.

Jason
AMONG THE
Israelites

On Tuesday, April the fourteenth, in the year 1462 BC, an extraordinary meeting took place on the eastern shore of the Red Sea. Two men met there. It would be no surprise that one of them was Moses, for on that date and in that place he is known to have led the Israelites through the parted waters of the sea. Standing alone on the shore watching these pilgrims arrive was a man named Jason. The exploits, adventures, and triumphs of that man along with his Argonauts are well known. Despite all the victories, Jason was a sad and lonely man at the time of his meeting with Moses. In sharp contrast, Moses stood in the midst of the crowd of his people. He had finally tasted a triumph of his own, first by freeing his people from bondage and then by leading them out of Egypt. The two men looked back to see columns of the Pharaoh's soldiers and chariots and horses entering into the sea's bedrock. And as they watched, a crashing noise came up as the walls of water rushed together swallowing the whole army. Jason was aghast. Moses smiled.

In the ensuing quiet, the two men studied each other. Then they began to share their stories. Moses, for his part, told of the long, long years of servitude his people had endured under the iron rule of the Pharaoh in Egypt. Jason explained the source of his profound grief: how his wife had murdered their two sons and his new wife-to-be, and how she suddenly disappeared.

Moses expressed sympathy for Jason, recognizing the pain of his grief. But he turned and looked at the mumbling and shuffling crowd. "We must begin our long trek, for we have a long way to go before we reach the Promised Land." He looked at Jason and asked, "Will you wish to join us?" Jason thought a moment, and then said, "I have nowhere else to go, so I might as well walk with you to this place you call Promised. We can talk as we walk." And at a signal from Moses, the crowd began to move.

As they walked, they discovered they had something in common. Both needed protection when they were very young. Jason as a boy learned that his father, the King of Iolkus, had been murdered and that his uncle, Pelias, had done it in order to claim the throne for himself. Jason's mother, fearing for his safety, sent him away into the mountains of Pelion, in the care of Cheiron, a centaur. Jason shrugged his shoulders, "Just as you see me now, isolated and alone by the sea, so was I growing up in the wilds of those mountains."

Moses responded, saying that he too had been protected. He thought for a moment and then recounted, "I was a baby, so I do not recall any of this, but I know that the Pharaoh in those days issued a decree that all male babies be killed in order to forestall a revolt that had been prophesied some few years into the future. So it was that my mother put me in a basket and hid me in the bulrushes of the Nile River. She also took pains to ensure that word of this reached the Pharaoh's sweet daughter, Bithia, and it was she who found me in those bulrushes. Out of pity she claimed me for her own. And so it was that I grew up in the royal household."

As they walked on, they came to a place where Moses stopped, letting others walk on past him. He and Jason stood by a large bush. Jason looked at the bush and at Moses and asked if that bush were important somehow. Moses reflected, "Yes. It marks an important moment in my life when I was still a young man."

He then told how he came to that bush. "One day, I saw a slave master flogging a poor defenseless Israelite slave. He was on the verge of killing the man. I was so outraged that I killed the master. Then I fled, putting my life of comfort behind me. I walked across the north end of the Red Sea and arrived here in front of this bush. Suddenly, I tell you, the bush burst into flames. An angel of the Lord spoke to me out of that burning bush and commanded me to return to Egypt and call on the Pharaoh to release the Israelites from their bondage. Even with the eloquent help of my brother Aaron, I could not persuade the man to let my people go."

"You seem to have done it now," said Jason, looking at the crowd.

"That is after God sent down on Egypt many plagues, plagues of frogs, gnats, locusts, skin boils, and others. All of them passed over the Israelites but brought great suffering to the Egyptians. one of them changed Pharaoh's mind. None, that is, until the tenth one."

"How was that different from the others?" asked Jason.

"It was much more severe. The Lord our God had announced that on a certain day at midnight, all firstborn children will die. He ordered us Israelites to feast on lambs and use the blood to mark our doors. The angel of the Lord would pass over those households while placing death on all other firstborn. I warned Pharaoh what was about to happen. He became angry and told me never to show my face in his court again. After it did indeed happen, he summoned me and ordered the release of the Israelites. And that is how it happened that we are here on this long trek."

When Moses had finished, he looked up and saw that the crowd was passing by and only stragglers were left. The two men rose and began to catch up with the crowd. Once they had done so, they resumed their conversation. Jason led off with a question: "Have you ever heard of the Golden Fleece?"

Moses replied, "No, never. But how could a fleece turn golden?"

Jason replied, saying, "It did not turn golden. It was gold." Then he went on to explain. "Our god, Zeus, once gave a distant ancestor of mine a golden ram. After many years the ram fell into the hands of Aietes, King of Colchis, who had it slaughtered and then hid the fleece in a sacred grove guarded by a dragon."

"Well, that is an interesting story, but what does it have to do with you?"

"I will tell you. I already told you that my uncle Pelias killed my father in order to take over his kingdom, called Iolkus. When I was a young man, I went to Iolkus to confront my father's murderer. When I arrived, I was ushered into a small chamber and told to wait. I waited there for what seemed a very long time. I was alone and I felt vulnerable. Suddenly out of a hidden door came King Pelias. He walked right up to me and stood over me. With a smirk on his face, he informed me that he was willing to relinquish the throne to me but only on one condition…."

Here Jason had to stop. The crowd had been slowing its pace and now three of them walked up to Moses. They spoke to him saying that they worry they will run out of food and water well before they arrive at that so-called "Promised Land." One of them added that they have now passed into a desert wilderness with no hope of refreshing supplies. Another complained about his sore feet. Moses replied saying simply that the Lord was with them and they shall not want. Grumbling among themselves, the three turned and resumed their walk.

Then Moses nodded and looked at Jason. "You were saying that King Pelias posed a condition. What was it?"

"First he made a point of reminding me that he could easily have me killed. (Of course, I was all too aware of that as I stood in that small chamber with no one in sight.) His condition required me to go to Colchis and to that sacred grove and bring him the Golden Fleece."

"Ha!" Moses exclaimed. "That's impossible. You'd be devoured by the dragon before you could even get close to the fleece."

"I did it!"

"You did it? How?"

"To start, the King generously provided me a great boat, the Argo, and a crew of men, who of course were dubbed Argonauts. So equipped, we set sail for Colchis on the Black Sea. I went to King Aietes demanding the whereabouts of the Golden Fleece. The King smiled and pointed the way to the sacred grove. He laughed at me as I started out, but his daughter, Medea, caught up with me and accompanied me to that place. There she amazed me with her magical powers. She put the dragon into a trance and magically lifted the Fleece into the air and flew it to me. I was so stunned by this that I turned to Medea in gratitude and wonder and took her into my arms. She used her powers and translated that gratitude into love."

"Aha!" said Moses nodding his head.

"You understand, I see. Well then, in the dark of night she and I and the Argonauts sailed away through the Bosporus, back into the Aegean. When we arrived in Iolkus, Medea worked another wonder, spontaneously giving birth to two young boys – not babies, but boys. The people of the city rose up against us. Out of fear and outrage against Medea and her sorcery, they threatened us, they rioted in the streets and threw stones. And so, again in the dark of night, we sailed away. I had to abandon any thought of claiming the throne, but I still had the Fleece and I took it to Corinth. King Creon had assured us of safe haven there."

Moses was becoming distracted while Jason was speaking and Jason himself slowed down almost to a stop. The crowd had begun to mill around, grumbling, complaining, even sobbing. Children wept. Then several men separated from the crowd and marched toward Moses. His brother, Aaron, also came to hear what these people were about to say. They stood in front of the brothers and finally began to speak. The first one growled, saying, "Where have you brought us? We are stuck here in this endless wilderness."

Another chimed in, "You two have no plan, no idea what you are doing!"

The third declared, "It would have been better if we stayed in Egypt. At least we always had something to eat."

And the fourth: "It would be better to die there than in this godforsaken place."

Moses held up his hand. "Listen to me, Israelites. Why do you accuse us? You are in God's hands. We all are. It was the Lord who delivered you out of Egypt and it is the Lord who is with us still."

Aaron stepped forward to address the crowd: "Have faith in the Lord, for He will bring deliverance. Follow where He takes us and you shall be rewarded...."

As Aaron spoke, Moses turned to Jason who was sitting on a rock rubbing his feet. "Will you continue with us as we follow where the Lord our God takes us?"

Jason looked up and shook his head. "I don't know anything about the lord your god. What I do know is that at one moment I was content, living in the good graces of King Creon. I gave him the Golden Fleece and he offered me his daughter, Glauce. I genuinely loved that woman. I distanced myself somewhat from Medea. Then suddenly Glauce was dead and so were my sons. I found out that Medea had killed our sons and sent a poisoned garment to Glauce. Medea herself disappeared. I was left alone in my grief." Jason kept talking but no one was listening. "And in that grief, I boarded the Argo and let the west wind blow wherever it might. When it foundered on rocks, I started walking, but the grief goes with me no matter where I go. It is with me now, here."

Aaron was still talking, assuring the people that the Lord will be with them and that He will provide meat and bread in the evening. Moses stepped up and said the people needed patience, love and faith, for they will all see the land of milk and honey."

Moses went on in that vein. Meanwhile, Jason stood and turned away. He began to walk in a northerly direction. No one noticed. He simply left the crowd. And no one of them ever heard of him again. As for Moses, he did finally see the Promised Land, but only from afar, standing on top of Mount Nebo. He died there without ever reaching the land himself.

Uriah THE HITTITE Appears•to David KING OF THE Israelites

The day had been quiet and languid. In the afternoon, David settled in his bed hoping a nap would restore his energy. After a fitful hour of tossing and turning, he gave up. Thinking a walk in the open air would dispel his lethargy, he climbed up to the roof of his palace and looked down at the spot where he had first caught sight of Bathsheba. The image of her at her bath came into his mind and desire rose within him. He turned and went down to the apartments where she and his several wives resided.

As soon as he entered her chamber, she rose and went to him and he held her in his arms. Then he felt her body shake, convulsed with powerful sobs. He led her to a couch and sat with her as she wept. She asked that he excuse her, for it had not been so very long since Uriah, her husband, had been killed in battle. David understood and he comforted her. He continued to hold her for the time it took her to regain composure. And he made love to her.

He stayed with her until she fell into a peaceful sleep. He listened to her gentle breathing and then he left. Making his way back to his quarters, he felt invigorated and pleased with himself. A voice in the back of his mind whispered a reminder that it was he who sent Uriah into battle. He did not listen to that voice, but went about his work. Indeed, he worked long into the night on royal administrative duties. Sleep came quickly this time.

As he slept, he seemed to see a figure moving toward him in a grey mist. At first it was just a silhouette. He heard a voice calling his name, "David…David…David." The figure was addressing him out of that mist and as the vapors lifted, he could make out it was Uriah looking straight at him. That silent confrontation seemed to last a long while. Finally, it was David who broke the silence: "What? What do you want? What?" Uriah kept staring at David. Then he said in a low, barely audible voice, "You think I don't know? You're wrong. I do know." Another pause followed and then David said, "What? What do you know?" Uriah smiled, saying, "You think that because I am a Hittite, the Lord will stay clear of me, that the Lord cares for no one unless the person is an Israelite? I know from the Lord what you have done. I know you have taken my wife. I know you tried to send me home, that you offered a place at your table, you tried to distract me. But I did not go home. Instead, I stayed with the army preparing for the siege of Rahbah. I know you had Joab, my commander, place me close and alone at the city walls. In that place you were sure I would be killed. And I was." David was alarmed. "How do you know these things?" Uriah said simply, "I know them through the Lord your God. When you awake, you will find Nathan before you and you will listen to him." So saying, Uriah faded into the gathering mist and disappeared.

King David awoke in a cold sweat. He looked around furtively. No one was there. He settled back. Deeply disturbed, he tried to put it all out of his mind. That could not have happened. It's all a dream. After a time, a voice seemed to say, "I am here." David sat bolt upright in his bed, "Who are you?" The man replied, "I am Nathan. You know me. I am sent to teach you a story." And Nathan told of a rich man who had a large flock of sheep but when he went to prepare a dinner for his guest, he snatched the only lamb belonging to a poor man.

When David heard the story, he exclaimed, "Why tell me such a story? You are teaching me a story, you say. What is there to teach? The rich man should be punished for what he did. He should die for that sin. The man should hang. Why tell me such a story?" Nathan replied simply, "You are that man." And he left.

Now as it happened, Bathsheba was with child. David reflected on Nathan's story. He began to worry. He recalled the ewe lamb and the rich man who stole it. As soon as the baby was born, David looked for signs that some calamity might happen. The child suddenly fell into a fever. David prayed that the child would live. He fasted and put on sackcloth and wept. For seven days he ate nothing and drank only water. Yet the baby only grew sicker. On the seventh day, he heard whispering among his attendants and he asked them if they were speaking of the child: "Is the child dead?" And they confirmed it.

Then David rose and cleansed himself, put on new clothes and ordered food to be placed before him. And he went to Bathsheba and comforted her in her grief. He sank into a contrite and painful state. He accepted what the Lord had done. He prayed the Lord would grant him a pure heart and create in him a steadfast spirit. He prayed in the Lord's house and ate in his own house. And he faced life for whatever it may bring.

Pontius Pilate

Accounts for Himself

(a monologue)

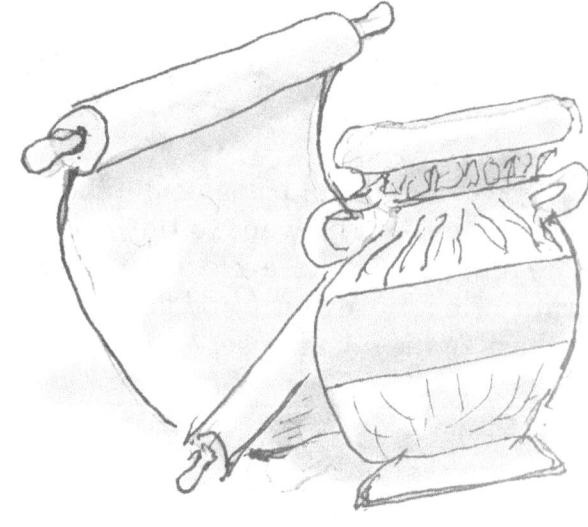

I would like to explain some things to you – things regarding my reputation. Almost every story about me makes me out to be muddle-headed and ineffective or else vile and vicious. Just to start with, my name is not Pilate. It is Pontius Pilatus from the Pontii family of central Italy. I served for ten years as Prefect and Governor of Judaea and they were ten years of pure exasperation. It was a post no one wanted, least of all myself.

You see, the imperial government of Rome is all based on patronage. You had to know someone to advance your career, someone with influence and willing to use it on your behalf. I had such a person – I thought. He was a member of the Patrician class and so very powerful. His name was Sejanus. He was kind enough to put my name forward for a post within the government. It was not enough. The Emperor Tiberius awarded the post to some pompous ass named Gaius Pamphilius. That is how I got this miserable appointment – Prefect and Governor of Judaea.

From the beginning I tried in every way to create peace in this alien and strange society. Naturally there was tension between the Jewish people and the Romans. The culture, the music, the religions are so very different. But I saw no reason why we could not exist together at the same time and in the same place. I don't mind telling you that I have nothing against the Jewish people. They can be very jolly and generous. I do find their leaders, the Pharisees, and especially the high priest Caiaphas, absolutely exasperating. They have a way of riling the people up into mass hysteria. My predecessor as Governor, Valerius Gratus, warned me about that. Indeed, soon after my arrival, the Augustan Imperial Cohort put up imperial standards bearing images of Caesar Augustus and Tiberius just outside the Temple in Jerusalem. The Jews rose up in a fury of protest against "graven images" and for five days they occupied the square in front of my palace. I finally managed to pacify them by removing the military unit and their standards to another post. For that Tiberius issued a decree of rebuke.

My worst day came about seven years into my reign on a particular Friday. I had been up very early that morning and had to sit in judgment of two thieves whom I found guilty and sent off to be crucified. I returned to my bed but a great noise went up outside my palace. I went out and there was that rabble-rouser, Caiaphas, with a mob of screaming Jews. They pushed a young man out in front declaring that he had blasphemed saying that he was the son of God. "For that he deserves death," they cried. "He claims to be a king and clearly that makes him an enemy of Caesar."

Now, I had one advantage. The Jews would not enter the home of a gentile for fear of defilement. That was why I used a stone slab (called Gabbatha) outside the palace to pass my judgments. So now I took the young man into the palace to interview him. He seemed a gentle and intelligent man but I could not get him to respond except to say that his kingdom was not of this earth. I thought that a peculiar thing to say, but it certainly was no crime. I went back out and told the mob that I found no fault in the man. But they screamed, "Crucify him! Crucify him!"

I took a chance at that moment. I reminded the crowd that it was Passover time and the tradition on that occasion has always been to find forgiveness and to free one captive from the prison. I asked them if they wished me to release this young man they had brought here. They screamed louder, "No! Crucify him!" Then: "We want Barabbas. Free Barabbas!"

I took another chance and had the young man flogged hoping that that would satisfy the people. I brought him out of the palace wearing a purple robe and a crown of thorns, the soldiers' way of mocking him. That would not do and they screamed again, "Crucify him!" I sat on my stone slab and washed my hands saying, "I will have nothing to do with this. Crucify him yourselves."

And they did. The same soldiers who flogged the man now took him away carrying the cross they would set up on Golgotha Hill, the hill of the skull, in order to crucify him along with the two thieves I condemned earlier. They left me sitting on the slab depressed and exasperated.

Late in the afternoon a strange darkness descended over the earth. It was frightening and then a powerful earthquake followed. It was as though the heavens, the earth and the universe itself were all in upheaval. I thought then that the man's claim to be the son of God might have been true. I wondered to myself, might I have stopped this? Could I have saved this young man?

Charon's
Complaint

Charon had a comfortable routine. Despite the dismal and repetitive nature of his work ferrying dead souls across the River Styx into Hades, it always gave him a feeling of accomplishment. He derived satisfaction from receiving shiny silver coins from the dead, even if he had to pry them out of their mouths. He loved silver coins, but what use he could find for them, no one knew. He also enjoyed using his great oar to beat recalcitrant souls into getting on board the ferry. Standing on the shore of the river one could hear the moans, sighs and weeping floating in the turgid air from the other side in Hades. Even that gave Charon a certain pleasure. Finally, he truly liked the acrid smell of the yellow mists that swirled around the river's edge. In short, he had no complaint.

Obviously, one day was very much like the last one. There really was no distinguishing day from night. It was always the same. Nevertheless, one day something would happen to jolt Charon out of his smug lethargy. It occurred after he had beaten a group of souls onto the ferry and pushed off into the lazy cross currents of the Styx. A ray of bright light suddenly pierced the darkness from above. Charon and everyone on the boat looked up. As they did, the ray grew larger and brighter. It created dazzling silhouettes of souls crowded together on the far side of the river. Into that vivid glow appeared a figure robed in brilliant white. The figure descended gently. It seemed to be a man holding out his hands in a gesture of generosity and acceptance. The spectacle had everyone transfixed, everyone, including Charon.

Then something even more astonishing happened. Before the figure touched the ground, the ray seemed to exert a powerful force that pulled a host of souls up and out of sight toward the source of the light. Each one seemed to rise up and move out of sight. Then Charon saw the figure turn toward his boat making the same welcoming gesture. Charon turned to look at his passengers. Suddenly several of them, at least a dozen, were pulled into the ray of light and they too disappeared. More and more left the ground and rose into the ray. It was astounding for all those left behind, particularly for Charon, who put aside his oar and sat down.

Then, as abruptly as it had appeared, the ray and the white clad figure vanished. The dark swirling mists re-appeared. For a long while, no one moved. In that stunned silence, Charon began to feel anger rise within him. He felt cheated, betrayed. "Who," he wanted to know, "was this interloper? What gives him the right to interfere in the affairs of Hell?" He felt robbed. It was his business and his pleasure to keep filling the deep dark circles of Hell. Now hundreds, maybe thousands, have been yanked from this rich and favored domain.

As time moved on, his red-hot anger turned into seething resentment. He watched other souls, some as soon as they boarded his ferry, rise up and disappear somewhere above. No one showed up with a shiny silver coin in hand or in the mouth. It was no longer fun to whack the dead souls with his oar to make them sit down in the boat. He made some inquiries and found out that the figure in question was a man who somehow took the sins of the world on his shoulders. Charon considered that simply gratuitous. What would be the point?

One day, as he pulled his empty ferry in from Hades' side of the river, he heard a hissing sound from somewhere on the riverbank. He looked around. At first he could see no one. After a while he spotted two glowing red eyes looking at him.

Another hiss sounded. "Hey, over here! I want to talk to you."

Very hesitantly, Charon approached the owner of those eyes, "Who are you? What's with all that hissing?"

"I am one who can help you."

"Why? You know something about that man who's stealing souls out of Hell? I tell you I'd like to kill the guy."

"Funny you should say that. They already killed him."

"Oh." Charon thought about that for a moment. "Then he ought to pay his fare here like every other soul."

"He's not exactly a soul. See, the third day after they killed him, he rose from the dead."

Now Charon was losing patience. "Who are you to come around here telling fairy tales? What nonsense!"

"I'll tell you who I am. Name's Satan. Like I said, I am here to help you. You may not be aware of this, but I am the one who sends you lost souls. I know how to play on the weakness of people. I put temptation in their path and you wouldn't believe how quickly they crumble. It's never long after that that they show up here at your ferry dock. That fellow who rose from the dead does everything he can to undermine my work. We're sworn enemies."

This was all news to Charon. He was dumbfounded. So much so that he sat down right there on the riverbank. Satan sat down with him and patted his shoulder. After a while, Charon turned to Satan and asked what he was offering to do. A bright white smile crossed over Satan's face under those glowing red eyes. "I'll tell what I'll do for you. I am going to redouble my efforts and I am going to send you more dead souls than you ever saw before. That's what I am going to do." Saying that, Satan stood up and gradually faded into the darkness above the river.

It was a while before Charon was aware that Satan had gone. He looked around and realized he was alone. He stood up and walked back to the ferry dock. Lost in thought he did not sense the arrival of another boatload of lost souls. He picked up his oar and went to work. Satan, too, seemed to be at work. Although it was never a case of "more souls than he had ever seen before," there was always a steady supply coming down the river's edge.

Nadab
metamorphosed

Nadab was still young but he had grown tired of tending sheep. He had been carrying his crook out in the pastures ever since he was a boy. There was a whole world of adventure waiting for him. One day, he decided it must be now or never. He handed his supervisor his crook and went to Haifa. He hoped to join the crew of a merchant ship that would take him to islands and ports beyond the horizon. At the harbor, he met a group of sailors who informed him that their ship would be putting out to sea the very next day and they were still hiring crew. It would be weeks before it returned to port and that meant he would see the world. He counted himself lucky to get a job on that ship. He was told to report the next day and pick up the provisions to be issued to him and be ready to sail.

Now, while his ship began its westward voyage, a ship was plying the waves of the Aegean and moving generally eastward. This was Odysseus' ship. After many months at sea, he had not found his way home to Ithaca. On this particular day he was approaching the island of Aeolia. This domain belonged to the god of the winds, Aeolus. Anyone attempting a sea voyage would naturally curry favor with this god, as well as with Poseidon, god of the seas. Since leaving Troy, Odysseus had his troubles with both gods. Poseidon had been especially vengeful, retaliating against Odysseus for having blinded his son, the one-eyed Cyclops. Odysseus thought it unlikely he could gain forgiveness from Poseidon but he was determined to pay homage to Aeolus.

As soon as the island of Aeolia came into view, the crew was impressed by its verdant and pleasant appearance, perhaps made possible by the fact that winds originate there but never blow onto the island itself. The closer the ship came to land, the more beautiful it seemed. Still, there was some trepidation about setting foot on the shore, not knowing how Aeolus would receive them. So as to ease their concerns, Odysseus said, "You stay here in case we need to make a hasty retreat. I'll go ahead to find this god, Aeolus." He did as he said and soon was out of sight.

A long wait ensued. It seemed as though hours had passed. Then a balmy breeze circled the men and caused them to look up. They saw Odysseus waving to them from the top of a hill. They took it to be a sign that they should follow him and so they did. He led them over hills and through valleys until they came to a resplendent white palace perched atop a high hill. Aeolus was standing at its grand portal waiting to welcome the men.

When everyone had arrived, Aeolus led them into a grand banqueting hall. When they were all seated at the tables, a feast magically appeared before their eyes. First came goblets of wine, then plates of vegetables, many roast pigs, followed by breads and varieties of desserts. Whenever a goblet became empty, it somehow refilled itself. Everyone was happy. During the feast, Odysseus and Aeolus moved aside and consulted on several issues. Among them was Odysseus' frustration in finding his way home to Ithaca. Quietly, Aeolus said he had a device that might help.

During this happy time, Nadab's ship had stopped at a number of ports and he had the rare chance of visiting cities he had only heard of before. He was assigned to manning a sail on one of the three masts. He enjoyed the work and the camaraderie of the crew—so different from keeping company with sheep.

While Odysseus' men were boarding the ship to leave the island of Aeolia, they noticed their leader accepting a large bloated bag from their host, Aeolus. They talked among themselves about what could be in such a full bag. Many thought it must be stuffed with gold. Actually, it was a bag of wind. It was to be used when nearing the waters of Ithaca to blow the ship into port. Until such time, Aeolus had warned, it must be kept closed.

The ship passed the island of the cannibals, the Laestrygonians, famous for killing and eating sailors. There was general rejoicing when the ship put the island behind it. Curiosity got the better of a few men who determined to open that bag they thought contained gold. As soon as they opened it, powerful winds blew in all directions causing the waters to mount up in great waves. The roiling of the waters also tossed Nadab's ship about and one huge wave nearly tipped the ship over which threw Nadab off the deck and into the sea. No one noticed. This would seem to be the end of Nadab, but suddenly the winds ceased to blow and the sea became calm. Nadab looked up and saw Odysseus' ship approaching him. He waved and cried out as loud as he could. He was saved and brought on board.

And so it was that Nadab joined the Greeks when they disembarked at the Island of Aeaea, home of the nymph goddess, Circe, famous as a sorceress. Some of the men were loath to get off their ship saying among themselves that they may have avoided the cannibals only to be bewitched. Circe, however, came to welcome them and to serve up a magical feast to rival the one created by Aeolus.

During the feast, Odysseus and Circe disappeared for a long while. Something happened between them that caused anger in her and she returned to the banqueting hall her eyes flashing a powerful energy that drove many of the men out of the building. Those who remained were suddenly transformed into pigs.

The squealing was loud with protest. The pigs ran this way and that and some left the building. Nadab was among them. In fact, he ran faster than any of the other pigs. Finally, he stopped running. He looked around and saw he was alone. He could hear the squealing in the distance. He was unsure whether it was better to stay away in isolation or to go back and join the others. He decided to stay put.

After a few days of running and rutting, he couldn't hear any more squeals. He returned to the palace and saw that the pigs had been restored to humans. Circe seemed to have reconciled with Odysseus and took pity on the men. That was all well and good for them, but Nadab remained a pig. In that form, he lived out the rest of his life as Circe's own pig on the island of Aeaea.

Greek Tourists *encounter* JESUS

In Athens' seaport town of Pireas, there once lived an entrepreneur by the name of Aristoteles Apelles. His many innovations were all part of his famous Double Alpha Touring Company. He organized multiple tours of the Mediterranean world. He designed and built a fleet of galley ships to transport clients to such places as Ephesus, Miletus, Cyprus, Damascus, Alexandria, Syracuse, Paestum, and as far as the Pillars of Hercules. Each galley ship had a crew of eighteen oarsmen who rowed to those exotic destinations with the help of a huge sail mounted on a thick mast. Above the heads of the oarsmen was a deck where the passengers could lounge while a gracious cruise attendant served food and drink. Finally, at the stern of each ship was a storage chamber for the tourists' luggage. At a discreet distance from it was a loo.

Very early one morning, before sunrise, the crew helped passengers board one of the galley ships. While they settled into chairs on deck, their luggage was being stowed. Another one of Aristoteles' remarkable innovations was the design of deckchairs that could be changed into sleep hammocks for long trips. The first destination was Cyprus which would require three nights on board. Some of the passengers were planning a visit to the island and return to Pireas on another galley ship.

The crew hoisted sail and took up their oars. As the sun came up over the eastern horizon, the ship left port. At set intervals, the oarsmen would raise their oars and allow the sail to do the work. Late on the fourth day the ship docked at Cyprus where it remained overnight. Early the next morning, it departed for Haifa.

Despite a strong westerly wind helping the ship along at a good speed, it was dark the next day when it arrived at Haifa. The passengers met Abobidiah, their tour guide who escorted them to an inn where they would spend the night. Abobidiah was a Jew who knew the land of the Hebrews well, understood comparative cultures, and spoke Greek fluently. That evening, he described the places they were about to see and the nature of the Jewish faith. Before adjourning, the group was astonished when Abobidiah reported a piece of news: "Here, right now in Israel, is a man claiming to be the son of God. For nearly three years he has been traveling throughout the land speaking in parables and working miracles. Many think him to be divine, perhaps descended from heaven. Others see him as the devil's tool. You will almost certainly hear people speak of him. His name is Jesus." The Greeks were amazed. They were used to gods coming to earth usually disguised as a swan or a bull or a cloud, but never as just a man walking among us.

After breakfast the following morning, the group gathered just outside the inn. They were told to bring their luggage and to wait for their conveyance to take them to the tour's first site. That conveyance would be another indication of Aristoteles Apelles' ingenuity. He had had carriages built expressly for touring. After a few moments, a pair of horses pulled the carriage up to the front of the inn amazing the Greeks. High on top were several seats facing forward. In the front next to the driver was a seat facing backward for the tour guide.

Underneath was a large enclosed space for all the luggage.

That afternoon they arrived in the city of Tiberias where they would remain for two days, long enough to visit several important sites. Among those was the palace built about a dozen years earlier by Herod Antipas (son of Herod the Great) to his own glory. Meanwhile, he paid tribute to Rome by naming the city after emperor Tiberius. They also visited the tomb of Maimonides and the Etz Chaim synagogue. In their leisure time, they enjoyed the spa at Hamat and the restaurants along the marina promenade.

The next day, they boarded a grand boat and sailed across the Sea of Galilee. Abobidiah pointed to the far shore where that fellow Jesus had taken two loaves of bread and a couple of fishes and created a feast for five thousand people. He also mentioned that the same Jesus was purported to have walked on the water of Galilee. One of the Greek passengers spoke up, asking the guide if he believed the man had really done those things. Abobidiah replied, "I do believe he did. Somehow those five thousand people got fed. There are eyewitness accounts of his walk on the water. He has created countless other miracles such as curing the sick, the blind, the crippled. Every day there are new reports. The authorities, the Pharisees and Sadducees, members of the Great Sanhedrin, are claiming it all to be the work of Satan. They are threatening drastic measures to force him to cease and desist."

The carriage was waiting for them when they left the boat. They began a journey southward along the east bank of the Jordan River. On the way, one tourist spoke up, asking, "Why should it matter to those authorities if this man walks about performing miracles? It's not hurting anyone." Abobidiah took in a long breath before answering. He said, "It upsets them to see the man pick up so many followers and violate so many of their laws. They especially don't like it when he declares himself to be the son of God. God, they say, doesn't have any sons. To make such a claim is blasphemy."

Their next major stop was to be Jerusalem, but it was a long journey requiring another overnight stay. The Greek tourists talked late into the night about how strange they find this Hebrew culture to be. They vest all power in these religious leaders who might arrest you at the drop of a hat.

Pushing onward early in the morning, they came to the town of Perea. Suddenly, Abobidiah had the driver bring the carriage to a full stop, startling the Greek tourists who looked around and saw nothing special. The guide pointed to a dozen men gathered to listen to the man facing them. "That is the man we have been talking about, the one who has done so many miracles. That's the one named Jesus." Everyone stared at the man expecting to see him perform another miracle. Nothing happened and the carriage went on.

After a short distance, they came to the town of Bethany. There they saw a large crowd watching some men carry a body wrapped in burial cloths out of a small house and into an adjacent cave. Two weeping women walked behind. After a while, the guide spoke softly about the deceased whom he had known as Lazarus, brother of the two women, Mary and Martha. He expressed some sorrow, for he knew the man had been very ill. After a respectful pause, the carriage moved on and soon arrived in Jerusalem.

The Greek party spent the next three and a half days in that wondrous city, visiting some of the surviving buildings of the City of David. More impressive was the temple built many years earlier by Ezra and Nehemiah on what was called the Temple Mount. It replaced the one built by King Solomon and destroyed by the Babylonians. Next to it was a gathering spot called Solomon's Colonnade. Solomon had erected an extensive and grand palace but that had fallen into ruins. Herod the Great built many new buildings and towers in his attempts to beautify the city. That included his own grandiose palace. He also built a retaining wall shoring up Temple Mount, expanding it to twice the size. One Greek joked that the Jews could save money over time: "They only had to build a single temple at a time while we Greeks are always putting up temples."

On the fourth day, they started the last leg of their journey, expecting to be back in Haifa by nightfall. Their route took them through Bethany again. Something strange was happening there and they came to a stop. A spectacle unfolded before their eyes. This was the same spot where they had seen Lazarus taken into the cave. Again, a crowd gathered, but this time the man named Jesus was talking with the two women they recognized as the sisters. Two or three men were rolling away the stone from the cave. After a few moments, they heard Jesus call, "Come out, Lazarus." There was a suspenseful silence. Out of that dark cave came a man shedding his shroud and burial cloths. The man was moving on his own. He was clearly alive. The sisters gasped while holding their scarves to their nostrils. The mourning crowd murmured with awe and wonder. The Greek tourists were amazed. They remained there until the sisters and Jesus took the man into the house. The crowd began to disperse and finally, the carriage went on.

The galley ship was waiting for them when they arrived back in Haifa. They were still in awe of what they had seen. At a loss for words, they struggled to say farewell to Abobidiah. Their tour of the land of the Hebrews had been unforgettable. It was not very long after their return to their homes in Greece, that they heard about the death of that man Jesus. The news came in bit by bit. They first heard that the authorities had prevailed on the Romans to arrest the man. Next, they heard that crowds took to shouting for his execution. The appointed Roman governor, a man named Pontius Pilate, tried to mollify the mob by having Jesus flogged. Flogging the poor man did not satisfy the mob. The last news reported the man was crucified. It was sad and difficult to accept. They did hear rumors that the man had risen from the dead, but they were dubious. If true, it would be a miracle greater than all the others.

The **HAIRY** *TWIN'S*

complaint

A Greek merchant ship lay in the harbor at Haifa for several days as it unloaded goods and took on more. During that time, the ship's crew had liberty to explore the city. Most of them knew the city, having served for years on this ship plying the waves of the Mediterranean with frequent stops at ports such as this one.

While in port, a group of sailors noticed something unusual. Every time they returned to the ship, they would encounter a strange man sitting on the pier, scowling and muttering under this breath. He seemed to be nursing some deep anger with an intensity that made them avoid him. On one occasion, however, they observed the ship's captain speaking with the man and exchanging papers. They guessed that the captain was recruiting him for the crew.

That new crew member was a Hebrew by the name of Esau. Esau was the firstborn son of Isaac and Rebekah, but he was the eldest only by minutes, for his twin brother tried to force his way ahead by grasping Esau's ankle and pulling him back to allow him to be the first the emerge from the womb. The story probably originated from observing how the two boys fought and grappled with each other as they were growing up. The parents often had to pull them apart. Even as adults, they indulged in fierce rivalry.

All this the sailors on board did not know. The next day after Esau was hired, the ship put out to sea heading for Cyprus. Of course, they now had to work with the man as they hoisted or dropped the ship's sails. He removed his shirt as he worked, revealing that he was uncommonly hairy about his shoulders, back and forearms.

As the days passed, the sailors became curious about this hairy Hebrew. It was difficult to elicit any information from the man who was taciturn and withdrawn. From time to time he would release a deep inner scream of anger. He tried to suppress it, only to have it emerge again. He spoke only in general terms about the source of his resentment and he often stopped in mid-sentence to take a deep breath. It seemed they would never get the whole story. Yet, they were able to ascertain that his brother Jacob had connived to deprive him of his patrimony and had taken his place as eldest son. Even his mother Rebekah had worked on the deception, taking advantage of his father's blindness. When he realized what had happened, Esau went into a towering rage and even threatened to kill Jacob. Hearing that, Rebekah sent Jacob away to her brother, Laban in Harran. Esau actually had no intention of killing his brother, but he left home planning never to return. That is how he came to Haifa looking for a ship to take him to distant lands.

Over the following days and weeks that the ship sailed on, some of the sailors befriended the hairy Hebrew. His anger slowly abated. He would join his new friends in various port cities. He got to visit those faraway places, places such as Ephesus, Tyre and Athens. This new interest began to awaken in him a feeling of peace that dispelled the anger that had consumed him for so long. He continued sailing back and forth for fourteen years.

At the end of that time, he felt the urge to return home. He hoped to find Jacob and make peace with him. In one corner of his mind he knew this was so unlikely as to be simply foolish. But he also sensed the need to test the possibility and perhaps regain a balance in his life.

Now, it so happened that over those fourteen years, Jacob worked on Laban's estate hoping to win approval to marry his daughter, Rachel. In the process he himself was deceived and, by a trick, found himself married instead to her older sister, Leah. He was promised, nevertheless, he could have Rachel also if he continued to work for Laban. That happened eventually and it happened over the same fourteen years that Esau was at sea.

Once back in his homeland, Esau began to search for his brother. He felt some trepidation that he might encounter Jacob and fall into the old habit -- fraternal warfare. He arranged for a large group of men to accompany him and be at the ready should the meeting turn sour. It took several days searching, but he came to place in a road where several people were coming toward him and he recognized the man at the front who was trying to rise from the ground. He was nursing a bad hip that made it difficult to rise. But he did raise his eyes and caught sight of his brother. At once he was on his feet summoning his men to come forward. In response, Esau spread his arms. This startled Jacob who had braced himself for battle. Esau went forward and, after a pause, threw his arms around his brother, who responded in kind.

They stood there weeping with joy. Jacob then turned to those who were behind him: his servants and their children, his wives, including Rachel and Leah, and his seven-year-old son. There were also sheep and goats, and Jacob offered some of them to Esau. Esau refused them and offered to travel together. Jacob agreed. They did so, even though from time to time Jacob took off in other directions, still unsure of Esau's good will. The family settled in Shechem, the very same place where they had been reunited, and lived there peacefully.